PEANUTS®

By **Charles M. Schulz** Illustrated by **Robert Pope**

Countdown to Halloween!

With a Story a Day

SIMON SPOTLIGHT
An imprint of Simon & Schuster Children's Publishing Division
New York London Toronto Sydney New Delhi
1230 Avenue of the Americas, New York, New York 10020
This Simon Spotlight edition July 2021
Peanuts and all related titles, logos, and characters are trademarks of Peanuts Worldwide LLC
© 2021 Peanuts Worldwide LLC.
See page 64 for individual copyright and writing credits.
All rights reserved, including the right of reproduction in whole or in part in any form.
SIMON SPOTLIGHT and colophon are registered trademarks of Simon & Schuster, Inc.
For information about special discounts for bulk purchases, please contact
Simon & Schuster Special Sales at 1-866-506-1949 or business@simonandschuster.com.
Manufactured in China 0421 SCP
2 4 6 8 10 9 7 5 3 1
ISBN 978-1-5344-8609-6 • ISBN 978-1-5344- 8610-2 (eBook)

October 1

Dear Great Pumpkin . . .

Linus was excited. It was October, and that was one of his favorite months of the year!

Why? Well, for one thing, he loved when the weather got a bit cooler, and he loved all the fall colors. He especially enjoyed watching the leaves change color on the trees and jumping in piles of leaves after they fell!

But there was one thing about October Linus loved most of all—Halloween!

And not for the usual reasons. You might think it was because he enjoyed trick-or-treating, or wearing a costume, or Halloween parties. No, Linus usually missed out on most of those things because he was waiting for the Great Pumpkin.

Linus believed that every Halloween, the Great Pumpkin picked the most sincere pumpkin patch he could find, and then visited it and left gifts for any good little boys and girls who waited in the pumpkin patch to see him.

Linus always wrote a letter to the Great Pumpkin and mailed it a few weeks before Halloween to say he was looking forward to Halloween and finally meeting him.

But it seemed to get more difficult every year, since none of his family or friends believed in the Great Pumpkin. His older sister,

Lucy, was especially a non-believer. She loved to tease him about the Great Pumpkin.

Linus took out a piece of paper and a pencil and began to write his letter.

Dear Great Pumpkin, I am looking forward to your arrival on Halloween night.

Just as he finished writing this sentence, Lucy came over and read what he wrote.

She smirked and said, "Santa Claus has elves to help him. What does the Great Pumpkin have, oranges? Ha ha ha!" Then she walked away, still laughing at her joke.

Linus sighed. He believed the Great Pumpkin was a lot like Santa, in that he knew which children were good and which were not.

Linus was worried that Lucy's joke might upset the Great Pumpkin.

He continued to write his letter, adding, *Please don't listen to my sister, Lucy, sir. Lately, her kind is everywhere.*

He signed his letter and sealed it in an envelope. He really hoped Lucy's joke wouldn't ruin his chances to see the Great Pumpkin this year!

A Story for

October 2

My Sweet Babboo!

Linus was taking a walk around the neighborhood on a very important mission. He was looking for the most sincere pumpkin patch he could find.

A sincere pumpkin patch didn't need to be large. It just needed to be made up of sincere pumpkins. And it couldn't have any sign of hypocrisy for as far as the eye could see.

Then Linus heard a familiar voice calling out to him.

"It's my Sweet Babboo!" Sally shouted as she ran toward him. "I am so happy to see you. It's like fate is telling us to be together!"

Linus rolled his eyes. "It's nice to see you too, Sally," he said, "but I'm not your Sweet Babboo."

"I was on my way to the library," Sally said, ignoring Linus. "What are you doing?"

"I'm looking for the most sincere pumpkin patch that I can find," Linus replied.

"And why are you doing that, my Sweet Babboo?" Sally asked.

"I'm not your Sweet Babboo," Linus said. "And do you mean to tell me that you don't know about the Great Pumpkin?"

Sally shook her head.

Linus stopped walking and turned to look at Sally.

"There are a lot of people out there who don't believe in the Great Pumpkin," he said. "But let me tell you what I believe."

He took a deep breath. "I believe that the Great Pumpkin exists. Every Halloween, he rises out of the most sincere pumpkin patch. Then he flies through the air, bringing toys with him for all the good children in the world!"

Linus closed his eyes for a moment. He imagined the Great Pumpkin with his giant bag of toys.

"That's what I believe," Linus said to Sally. "What do you think?"

Sally was quiet for a moment. Then she smiled.

"Well, Sweet Babboo, here's what I think," she said.

Linus leaned in eagerly. "What is it?" he asked.

"I think my Sweet Babboo has very nice eyes!" Sally said dreamily.

"Aaugh!" Linus yelled. "I am not your Sweet Babboo!"

October 3

Things Could Get Lost in a Pumpkin Patch

Snoopy was curious about Linus's stories about the Great Pumpkin. He agreed to go to the pumpkin patch with Linus and check it out.

Linus brought Snoopy to the center of a huge pumpkin patch. "Isn't it wonderful, Snoopy?" Linus said. "Every year I try to find the most sincere pumpkin patch imaginable. There is no way anyone can find a pumpkin patch more sincere than this one! It's magnificent."

Snoopy looked around. Frankly, he was a little disappointed.

This is it? He thought. *All I see are a bunch of pumpkins. I thought at least there would be a band playing or someone handing out something fun to eat like cupcakes!*

Linus sighed happily. "So on Halloween, the Great Pumpkin is going to appear right here and give treats to all the good boys and girls waiting for him."

He paused for a second and looked at Snoopy. "I'm sure he'll have treats for any dogs that wait for him too," he added.

Well, I certainly hope so, Snoopy thought. *If I'm going to miss trick-or-treating and Halloween parties, I'd better be rewarded.*

Linus had a dreamy look on his face. "I just know this is going to be the year, Snoopy," he said. "I am finally going to meet the Great Pumpkin. What should I do? What should I say? Should I shake his hand? Do I call him 'Great Pumpkin' or 'Mr. Pumpkin'? Should I give him a hug? Do you think he'd mind if I hugged him?

"I think I'll be so excited about meeting him, I won't be able to control myself! What do you think, Snoopy? Snoopy, are you listening to me?"

Snoopy wasn't listening. He was looking around the pumpkin patch.

Good grief, something small could get lost very easily around here, he thought. *If I bring Woodstock here, I'd better keep an eye on him. He could get lost, and I'd never see him again!*

Linus smiled at Snoopy. "I see you're looking around at everything," he said. "You must love this pumpkin patch just as much as I do!"

October 4

I Was Never Here

One Halloween, Linus and Snoopy were waiting for the Great Pumpkin.

"Thank you for coming with me, Snoopy," Linus said. "I do this every year, and I'm usually by myself. It gets kind of lonely."

Snoopy didn't answer. He was thinking of all the places he'd rather be. Trick-or-treating with his friends. Dancing at a Halloween party. Watching a scary movie on TV. Winning first prize for the best Halloween costume.

But Linus was a very good friend. Snoopy wanted to help him out.

And who knows, Snoopy thought. *Maybe we really will see the Great Pumpkin!*

And that would be the best story of them all.

But the night dragged on and there was no Great Pumpkin in sight. Snoopy's stomach grumbled.

I should have brought some snacks, he thought. *If the Great Pumpkin does show up, will he bring a pizza?*

It was getting a little chilly too. Snoopy looked over at Linus.

At least he has a blanket! Snoopy thought.

Linus looked over at Snoopy, and it was as if he read Snoopy's mind. He wrapped the blanket around his shoulders and motioned for Snoopy to join him. Snoopy snuggled in.

Suddenly, Linus and Snoopy both heard noises and laughter. They looked at each other. Could it be? Was the Great Pumpkin finally here?

But then as the laughter grew closer, they realized it was just a bunch of kids treat or treating nearby who were passing the pumpkin patch.

"Sorry, Snoopy," Linus said. "I guess it was a false alarm." He looked closer at Snoopy. "Hey, Snoopy," he said. "Are you wearing sunglasses? Is that part of a Halloween costume?"

Snoopy looked over at Linus in his big black movie-star sunglasses.

There are some places where you don't want to be recognized, he thought. *And this pumpkin patch is one of them. If anybody asks, I was never here!*

October 5

Get the Name Right!

Rrring! It was the end of the school day. Marcie closed her notebook.

Peppermint Patty raised her fists in the air. "Yes! Class is finally over!" she said.

Then she turned to Marcie. "I called you last night, but you didn't answer the phone."

"Sorry, sir," Marcie said. "My dad took me to my first hockey game last night."

Peppermint Patty's eyes lit up. She loved all kinds of sports, including hockey.

But then Marcie began to talk on and on about the Zamboni that kept the ice smooth for the games.

"What about the hockey players?" Peppermint Patty interrupted. "Did they play well?"

Marcie nodded. "It's amazing how fast the players skate up and down the court—"

"Rink," Peppermint Patty corrected. "It's an ice rink."

"Right," Marcie said. "Oh, and next week my dad is taking me to a basketball rink!"

Peppermint Patty laughed. Marcie had never been very good about paying attention to sports!

After saying goodbye to Peppermint Patty, Marcie began walking home. She saw Linus walking up ahead. She walked faster to catch up to him.

"Hello, Marcie! How are you?" Linus said.

"I'm good," Marcie said.

Then Marcie remembered something that Lucy had recently said about Linus.

"May I ask you something?" she asked him.

"Sure, Marcie," Linus said. "What is it?"

"Have you been able to see the Great Squash yet?" Marcie asked.

Linus tried to keep quiet, but he just couldn't.

"It's not the Great Squash—it's the Great Pumpkin!" he yelled in exasperation.

"Oops, sorry," Marcie said quickly. "Well, I'd better hurry home. I want to watch the hockey match on TV tonight! First pitch is at seven o'clock!" She hurried away from Linus.

All Linus could do was shake his head.

October 6

The Perfect Halloween Treat

Lucy was discussing Halloween with her youngest brother, Rerun. "You are finally old enough to really enjoy Halloween," she told him.

Rerun was thrilled. He loved doing things with his older brother and sister, and always felt sad when there was something he couldn't do. So he was excited to share Halloween with Lucy.

"What happens? What do I do?" Rerun asked.

"Well, first you need to get a costume. You can dress up as anything you want!" Lucy said.

"Anything?" Rerun said. "Can I be a cowboy?"

"Of course!" Lucy cheered. "I will help put your costume together for you. You will make a great cowboy!"

"What else should I know about Halloween?" Rerun asked.

"We go knock on our neighbor's doors," Lucy said. "And when they open the door you have to say, 'Trick or treat!'"

"Why?" Rerun asked.

"Because people are supposed to give you something, or you might play a trick on them," Lucy explained. "But don't worry, all our neighbors will give you things."

"Things? People give us things?" Rerun said, surprised. "What kind of things? Like a new bicycle?"

"No, mostly candy," Lucy said. "Sometimes gum. Sometimes a quarter."

"I'd rather have a new bicycle," Rerun said. "I can't ride to school on a stick of gum!"

"We have to get you a big bag or Halloween bucket to hold all your treats," Lucy said. "Wait a minute."

She looked in the hall closet and came out with a large bag that said "Trick or Treat" on it. She handed it to Rerun.

"Here you go," she said. "This should be big enough for everything people give you."

Rerun looked at the bag doubtfully.

"What's the matter?" Lucy asked. "Don't you like the bag? Look, it even says 'Trick or Treat' on it!"

"I don't know," Rerun said.

"What don't you know?" Lucy asked.

"I don't think a new bicycle will fit in this bag!"

"Good grief!" Lucy said.

A Story for

October 7

Practice Makes Perfect

Rerun was excited about trick-or-treating for the first time. Lucy decided he needed a little practice first. She handed him a brown paper shopping bag.

"What's this for?" Rerun asked.

"I want you to practice your trick-or-treating skills," Lucy said. "Now, pretend we are at someone's front door. What do you do?"

"Ring the doorbell?" Rerun guessed.

"Yes, and then what?" Lucy asked.

Rerun wasn't sure, so he took another guess. "I say, 'Hi! Nice weather we've been having lately?'"

Lucy groaned. "No, no, no! You just say 'trick or treat' and hold up your treats bag, so they can give you something."

"That's all I say? 'Trick or treat'?" Rerun asked. "It seems a little bit rude."

Lucy sighed. "It's okay. It's tradition. It's what people are expecting you to say. You can say 'Thank you,' after they give you a treat, if you want to be polite. Okay, now let's go."

"Go where?" Rerun asked, confused.

"Trick-or-treating," Lucy said.

Now Rerun was really confused. "But it's not Halloween yet," he said.

"I know, silly," Lucy said. "Don't worry. We are just going to one house, and it's just for practice. I want to see how well you do when you have to ring a real doorbell."

Lucy brought Rerun to Charlie Brown's house. He rang the doorbell perfectly. Charlie Brown's sister Sally opened the door.

"Hi, Sally," Lucy said. "My brother is practicing for Halloween."

Sally nodded. "Okay," she said.

Rerun gulped. He looked at Lucy, and then back at Sally. "I forgot the words!" he said.

"No treat for you!" Sally said. "Come back when you remember them!" Then she slammed the door shut.

Lucy looked at her little brother. Then she put her arm around him.

"Okay, clearly you need a little more practice," she said.

October 8

The Perfect Costume

Snoopy and Woodstock were laying on the doghouse thinking about their Halloween costumes. It was only a day away and they didn't have anything ready!

Woodstock chirped up with an idea. He flew inside the doghouse and pulled out a sheet.

Snoopy shook his head. They were ghosts last year! They couldn't wear the same costume twice.

This year, Snoopy was determined to have the spookiest costume of all. He and Woodstock always won the Halloween costume contest.

The two friends spent the rest of the afternoon brainstorming ideas for their costumes. They could be pumpkins, or mummies, or wizards!

Snoopy sighed. *None of those are scary enough,* he thought.

Finally as night fell, they agreed to think about it some more in the morning.

Snoopy sat up watching the night sky. Against the full moon, Snoopy saw a bat flying overhead.

One of us needs to stay awake in case of vampires, he thought. *That's it!*

Snoopy suddenly had a great costume idea. He snuck around Woodstock, who was sleeping silently, and got to work.

First, he went into the round-headed kid's house and pulled out a few pieces of clothes. Then he took the sewing machine over to his doghouse and began creating the perfect Halloween costume, careful not to wake Woodstock in the process. He wanted to surprise his best friend.

In the morning, Snoopy waited patiently for Woodstock to wake up. As soon as he did, Snoopy barked, *Happy Halloveen!* He was a vampire!

Woodstock howled with laughter. He laughed so hard he fell from the doghouse. Woodstock thought Snoopy looked funny, not scary!

Snoopy hung his head. *Now Halloween is ruined,* Snoopy thought. He walked over to the park sadly.

Then Woodstock chirped loudly beside him. Snoopy looked up and saw that his friend was wearing . . . his own vampire costume!

The two vampires hugged and made the final touches to their costumes and to the doghouse.

Halloween wasn't about having the perfect costume, it was about having fun with friends! Snoopy and Woodstock were ready for *Halloveen!*

A Story for

October 9

Choosing a Costume Is Hard

Charlie Brown and his sister Sally were walking home from school. Sally looked a little worried.

"What's wrong, Sally?" Charlie Brown asked.

"Everyone in my class was talking about Halloween costumes. I haven't thought of anything to wear yet. I'm not sure I like costumes," Sally said.

"What?! Costumes are the *best* part of Halloween!" Charlie Brown exclaimed. "It's the only time of the year you can be anyone or anything! You can dress up as a dragon! You can dress up as a ghost! You can be an astronaut! Anything!"

"Really?" Sally asked. "I can be anything?"

"Yes! I'll help you. Just try on a few different things, and I'll let you know if they're a good costume," Charlie Brown said.

When they got home, Sally went into her room and thought about what her brother said.

Then she started pulling various things out of her closet. She tied a scarf around her head and put on her favorite tie-dye shirt. Then she stepped out into the hallway to show her brother.

Charlie Brown looked at her for a while and then said, "I'm not sure this really says 'Halloween.'"

Sally went back into her room and put a sheet over her head. She stumbled out of her room.

Charlie Brown clapped. "That's perfect!" he said happily.

But Sally didn't feel perfect. She couldn't see! Plus, she didn't like ghosts, so how was she supposed to act like one for the entire night?

Sally went to sleep and kept thinking about what she wanted to be most in the world.

In the morning she knew exactly who that was. She put on her "costume" and went over to the kitchen for breakfast.

Charlie Brown came out in his mummy costume. He looked her up and down and asked, "Why aren't you wearing your ghost costume to school? It's Halloween! Who are you supposed to be?"

Sally pointed to the S initial on her sweater. "I'm Super Sally!" she said. "I thought about what you said, and there's no one I would rather be than me!"

"Good grief!" said Charlie Brown.

But then he smiled. He thought Sally's costume was super!

October 10

Lucy Surprises Schroeder

Last October, Lucy couldn't wait for Halloween. The only problem was she couldn't decide what her costume should be.

I'm always a witch, Lucy thought. *How boring! Plus, this year I want to dress up as something completely different.*

"I know what you should be, Lucy," Linus told his sister. "You should dress as the Great Pumpkin!"

"Don't be ridiculous!" Lucy shouted. "I'm not going to dress up as something that doesn't even exist!"

Schroeder was practicing the piano when Lucy stopped by.

"Schroeder!" Lucy said. "What should I be for Halloween?"

"Sorry, Lucy," Schroeder replied. "I need to practice my new piano piece. It was written by the late, great Ludwig van Beethoven. One of the greatest composers of all time."

"No one cares about Halloween but me!" Lucy yelled.

She left Schroeder's house and went back home to think.

What can I be that will truly be the best costume ever? Lucy thought. *I want to be something really great!*

Suddenly, Lucy remembered something Schroeder had said.

Wait a minute! I can dress up as Beethoven! Schroeder said he is one of the greatest composers of all time! That means that I will have one of the greatest costumes of all time!

A few days later, it was Halloween.

Lucy couldn't wait to show her friends her costume. Especially Schroeder!

Schroeder looked happier than Lucy had ever seen him. He had a huge smile on his face.

"Who are you supposed to be?" Charlie Brown asked.

"Are you dressed as my grandma?" Sally asked.

Suddenly, Schroeder spotted Lucy from across the room. He rushed to her side.

"This is indeed the best costume I have ever seen," he said. "Lucy is dressed as the late, great Ludwig van Beethoven!"

Schroeder looked happier than Lucy had ever seen him. He had a huge smile on his face.

Lucy beamed. She was hoping Schroeder would recognize her very great costume and he did!

October 11

Pigpen Surprises Linus

Linus knew everyone thought it was silly for him to believe in the Great Pumpkin. But he knew someday there would be one Halloween when he would finally meet the Great Pumpkin and prove his existence to everyone.

But in the meantime, life was hard. He was going to miss out on Halloween parties. Again. He was going to miss out on trick-or-treating. Again.

Linus's friend Pigpen was over for a visit. He was trying to cheer Linus up.

"Why don't you just take a break from the pumpkin patch, just this once?" Pigpen asked. "If the Great Pumpkin is as nice as you say he is, I'm sure he'll understand. Halloween only comes once a year, and I'm just saying, maybe you should think about, just this once—"

"Noooo!" Linus said, and he covered his ears with his hands. "Stop saying that!" Pigpen rushed out of the room.

A few minutes later, alone in his room, Linus decided the only thing that would make him feel better would be to write another letter to the Great Pumpkin right away.

Dear Great Pumpkin,

I am looking forward to your arrival. Soon you will rise out of the pumpkin patch and fly through the air. I have tried to be good all year long, and I hope that you will bring me lots of presents.

Suddenly, Linus heard someone cough. He turned around, and Pigpen was standing behind him, reading over his shoulder.

Linus braced himself, waiting for Pigpen to tease him. But then Pigpen said the most surprising thing Linus had ever heard.

"Will you put in a good word for me, too, Linus?" Pigpen asked. "I've tried to be good too."

Linus broke out in a huge grin.

If Pigpen was starting to believe, anything was possible! Linus quickly put in a good word for Pigpen, and mailed his letter. He couldn't wait for Halloween night.

October 12

Linus Has a Bad Day

Linus couldn't understand why no one was interested in the Great Pumpkin. He walked up to a neighbor's house and knocked on the door. The door opened and a woman answered.

"Good afternoon, ma'am," Linus said politely. "I'd like to tell you about the Great Pumpkin!" The door immediately slammed in his face.

Linus took a deep breath and knocked on another door. This time a teenage boy answered.

Linus smiled brightly. "Hi!" he said. "Would you like to hear about the Great Pumpkin?"

"No!" the boy yelled, and he slammed the door too!

Linus sighed. *I'll give it one more try,* he thought to himself.

He knocked on a third door. A little girl answered.

Once again, Linus smiled widely and said, "Hi! Would you like to hear about the Great Pumpkin?"

"Nooooooo!" the little girl yelled. She also slammed the door.

Linus decided to go home and write to the Great Pumpkin.

Dear Great Pumpkin,

I've been trying to tell more people about you, but nobody wants to listen. I had three doors slammed in my face today. But do not worry, I will never stop believing in you.

Sincerely,

Your friend, Linus van Pelt

As Linus walked to the mailbox, he started to feel a little bit better.

Soon it would be Halloween, and he would meet the Great Pumpkin. And then all those people who slammed doors in his face would be sorry!

Linus walked up to the mailbox and dropped his letter in. He gave a happy sigh when all of his sudden his fingers slipped and . . .

SLAM!

Even the mailbox slammed in his face!

This just isn't my day, Linus thought. *Halloween better hurry up and get here fast!*

A Story for
October 13

Lucy and Rerun Are Good Siblings!

It was Rerun's first Halloween ever, and he was all ready!

"Well, how do I look?" Rerun asked Lucy.

He stood in front of her in his Halloween costume. He was dressed as a cowboy.

"You look great!" Lucy said. "How do I look?"

She was dressed as a queen, and she touched her shiny crown.

"You look great too," Rerun told her. "Very royal." He held up a large bag. "Here's the bag I'm going to put all my treats in."

Lucy looked at the sack. She nodded. "That's a nice big bag," she said. "Perfect. Now don't forget, when the door is opened, give them your biggest smile when you say, 'Trick or treat!' Hey, maybe you should tell them this is your very first time trick-or-treating! They may even give you extra candy. Okay, let's go. But there's one thing we have to do first. Follow me."

Rerun followed Lucy into the pumpkin patch, where Linus was already waiting for the Great Pumpkin.

"Linus, we're going trick-or-treating. Are you sure you don't want to come with us?" Lucy asked.

"No, thank you," Linus said politely. "I'm waiting for the Great Pumpkin."

Lucy rolled her eyes. "Fine," she said. "But don't expect us to share our treats with you! Come on, Rerun."

As Lucy and Rerun left, Rerun suddenly looked at Lucy and broke out in a huge smile.

Lucy stared at him. "What are you smiling about?" she asked.

"Now I know why you keep telling me to get lots of candy," Rerun said. "We're going to give some to Linus, aren't we?"

Lucy nodded. "Yes, you're right," she admitted. Then she looked at Rerun. "And if you tell anyone, I'll tie you to a tree with your own lasso, cowboy!"

Rerun grinned. "Don't worry, big sister," he said. "I love Linus too. Your secret is safe with me."

He lifted up his trick-or-treat bag. "Okay, now let's go out and get some delicious candy for you, me . . . and Linus!"

October 14

Spreading the Word

Charlie Brown had just finished breakfast when he heard a knock on the front door.

Linus was standing on the porch with a determined look on his face.

"I really need your help, Charlie Brown," Linus said.

He planned to go from door to door, telling everyone in the neighborhood about the Great Pumpkin.

But there was a problem. Linus was just one person, and there were so many houses to visit by himself.

That's why Linus also really needed his friend Charlie Brown to help him out so that everyone in the neighborhood could hear about the Great Pumpkin.

Linus could visit all the houses on the left side of the street, and Charlie Brown could visit the houses on the right.

"But I'm no good at this kind of thing," Charlie Brown said, shaking his head nervously.

"Please help me, Charlie Brown! People have to learn about the Great Pumpkin!" Linus begged.

"Okay." Charlie Brown sighed and took a deep breath.

Then he walked up to the first house on the right side of his street. It was decorated for Halloween with big spiderwebs and mean-looking zombies.

Charlie Brown gulped and turned around. Maybe he would come back to this house later.

The next house was painted a pretty shade of blue, and a welcome sign hung on the door. This house seemed like a better place to visit first.

Charlie Brown smoothed his shirt and cleared his throat. He counted to three and then rang the doorbell.

"G-good morning," Charlie Brown said. "I'm here to tell you about the Great Pumpkin. On Halloween night, the Great Pumpkin rises out of the pumpkin patch and brings toys to all the children in the world!"

Charlie Brown beamed. He did it! He had rung a doorbell and talked about the Great Pumpkin, just like Linus had asked him to do!

Charlie Brown turned around and walked away from the house.

Boy, was he glad that no one answered the door. That would have been embarrassing!

A Story for
October 15

A Costume for Woodstock

Snoopy was getting a little impatient with Woodstock. Woodstock still hadn't picked out his Halloween costume.

Halloween is one of the best nights of the year, Snoopy told him. *You can dress up as anything you want! It's fun!*

Woodstock wasn't so sure.

At first he tried a ghost costume, but no matter how much he cut the sheet, it was still too big, and he kept tripping over it. He tried a witch costume, but the broom was too heavy for him to carry all night. He tried a scary monster costume, but it was so scary, he frightened himself a little!

Snoopy, on the other hand, loved to dress up! He showed Woodstock a few of his favorite costumes.

He came out wearing a tuxedo and dark sunglasses. *I'm a movie star!* Snoopy said. Then he came out wearing a uniform and holding a baseball bat. *Now I'm a world famous home run hitter,* he told Woodstock. Snoopy came out of his doghouse a third time, holding a painter's palette and wearing a beret and a smock. *Now I'm an artist,* he said. *Would you like me to paint your portrait?*

Then Snoopy came out of his doghouse one more time. He was wearing bathing trunks and carrying a surfboard!

Cowabunga! Snoopy shouted. *I'm a champion surfer! It's time to hit the waves.*

Woodstock cheered. He thought Snoopy looked fantastic in any costume.

Snoopy sighed. *I give up,* he told Woodstock. *I don't know what else to tell you except to maybe think of something or someone you love, and then dress up as that for your costume.*

Woodstock thought for a moment and then broke out in a huge smile. He went in Snoopy's doghouse for a while, and then came out in his costume. He decided to dress up as someone he loved very much—Snoopy!

October 16

Dear Ms. Great Pumpkin!

Linus was discussing the Great Pumpkin again with Franklin and Sally. It turned out his friends were very curious about the Great Pumpkin.

"What do you think the Great Pumpkin is like?" Franklin asked.

Linus thought for a moment before answering.

"I'm sure he's smart and kind," he said. "And funny and thoughtful. I know whatever gifts he leaves for me will be just exactly what I want, because he wants to make sure every girl and boy who believes in him is happy."

"What does he look like?" Sally asked.

"I'm not sure," Linus said. "But I bet he has a great smile and kind eyes."

"How old is he?" Sally asked.

"I don't know," Linus said. "But I think he's been around forever, like Santa Claus. He's ageless!"

"Do you think he's handsome?" Sally asked.

"I don't know that either, but it doesn't really matter," Linus said.

"I bet he's not as handsome as you are, Linus," Sally said dreamily.

"Oh, good grief," Linus groaned.

Just then Lucy walked by. She had been listening to the entire conversation.

"Hmmm," she said. She smiled mysteriously at all three of them.

"What do you mean by 'hmmm'?" Linus asked Lucy. "What are you thinking?"

Lucy stared Linus straight in the eyes.

"You keep asking, 'What does he look like, how old is he, is he handsome?'" Lucy said.

"So?" Linus said.

Lucy leaned in close to Linus's face.

"How do you know the Great Pumpkin isn't a *she*?" Lucy asked.

Linus, Franklin, and Sally all gasped!

"Ha! It never even occurred to you, did it?" Lucy said triumphantly as she walked away.

LInus couldn't stop thinking about it. What if Lucy was right and the Great Pumpkin was a she? Linus decided to write a new letter, start it with "Dear Ms. Great Pumpkin," and mail it right away. He wasn't taking any chances!

A Story for
October 17

Halloween Means Scary Stories

Snoopy and Woodstock were camping with the Beagle Scouts for the weekend. They went on a hike in the morning, took a nap by the lake in the afternoon, and then walked over to their campfire in the evening. There was nothing like spending time outside and enjoying the fresh autumnal air!

The scouts were roasting marshmallows over the fire and enjoying warm cups of hot milk. Everyone was happy.

Woodstock chirped at Snoopy. He wanted Snoopy to tell a spooky Halloween story.

Snoopy wasn't sure. *The scouts usually don't like to get scared,* he thought.

Woodstock kept chirping for a scary story.

Snoopy looked around at the scouts. He did think they looked a little too comfortable. He finally agreed and pulled out his trusty old book of Halloween stories. He had the perfect one—not too scary, but spooky enough to get into the Halloween spirit!

Snoopy cleared his throat and then began to read.

Once upon a time, there lived an old dog named Shadow. He lived in a large doghouse next to an abandoned mansion. Every Halloween, Shadow locked himself up in his doghouse and didn't dare to come out. He had heard stories of ghosts and goblins coming out of the mansion on Halloween night. He didn't want to see them or for them to see him.

But on one Halloween, Shadow heard the crunch, crunch, crunch of leaves outside his doghouse. Just as he sat up, he heard a rustling on his doorknob . . .

Snoopy suddenly looked up from his book to find that the scouts were gone! *Where is everyone?* he thought.

Woodstock chirped loudly from behind, and as Snoopy turned around, he felt something heavy on his head. The scouts were crouched on Snoopy's head, trembling.

I guess my story was too *scary,* Snoopy said. *Okay, no more stories! Let's toast some more marshmallows!*

The scouts cheered!

A Story for
October 18

A Misunderstanding

Linus and Snoopy were tired. They had been exploring different pumpkin patches all day long.

When they reached the last one, Snoopy immediately stretched out for a nap.

Who knew exploring pumpkin patches would be such hard work? he thought.

"I know you're tired, Snoopy," Linus said. "I'm tired too. But you know we needed to look at every pumpkin patch to make sure the one we chose was the most sincere." He looked around the pumpkin patch. "I think we saved the best for last. This one looks perfect to me! What do you think?"

Snoopy looked up sleepily. *I think this pumpkin patch looks like every other one we've looked at for the last three hours!* he thought. But whatever made Linus happy was fine with him. Snoopy nodded.

Linus clapped. "Great! This is the one!"

Snoopy nodded again, then grabbed a tiny pumpkin and placed it under his head to use as a pillow. *Now it's finally time for a quick snooze,* he thought and closed his eyes.

But suddenly the sound of a girl yelling startled both Snoopy and Linus. "Hey, you two! Get out of here, or I'm calling the police!"

Snoopy panicked and hid behind Linus.

The girl ran up to Linus. "Gotcha!" she shouted. "Don't even think about trying to run away! I am faster than you, and I will catch you every time. So stay right where you are, thief!"

She glared at Linus. She wasn't kidding around. She was really angry at him.

Linus was confused. "Thief? I don't understand," he said. "What have I done? I'm just trying to pick the most sincere pumpkin patch to wait for the Great Pumpkin! I would never steal anything—otherwise the Great Pumpkin may not come and bring me anything on Halloween night!"

Now it was the girl's turn to look confused. "Most sincere pumpkin patch? Great pumpkin?" the girl said. "Kid, I don't know what you're talking about, but I guess it's okay. I thought you were stealing pumpkins! Okay, carry on. Happy Halloween!"

October 19

Go Away!

Linus realized he hadn't been able to convince anyone that the Great Pumpkin was real, and the Great Pumpkin was probably very sad.

That night, Linus wrote the Great Pumpkin a letter.

Dear Great Pumpkin,

I know you must be sad that I haven't gotten anyone else to believe in you. I have been trying very hard, but I promise to try even harder.

As a matter of fact, I am going to visit some of my neighbors tomorrow and tell them about you. I'm sure they will be very interested, and by the time Halloween is here, you will see a pumpkin patch filled with new friends.

I am looking forward to meeting you soon.

Sincerely,

Linus van Pelt

Linus mailed his letter, and later that night, he dreamed he was in a pumpkin patch filled with happy, smiling people, all cheering for the Great Pumpkin. When he woke up, he was determined to make his dream come true!

It was Saturday, and so right after breakfast, Linus decided to visit some of his neighbors. He picked a pretty house with a bright white door and a big pumpkin on the porch.

Linus thought the pumpkin was a good sign. He rang the doorbell.

"Go away!" a girl's voice yelled.

But Linus was determined to talk to someone new about the Great Pumpkin.

"Hello?" Linus shouted back. "I'd just like to speak with you for a few minutes—"

"You had better leave right now!" the voice shouted. "Or I'm sending my dog out to get you!"

Now Linus was nervous! He wanted to talk about the Great Pumpkin, but at the same time, he didn't want to get bitten by a dog.

"Okay, okay! I'm leaving!" Linus said hurriedly. "I'm sorry to have bothered you."

Suddenly, a girl peeked out the front door.

"Hi," she said.

"Hi," Linus said back. "I'm sorry to have bothered you. Please don't have your dog bite me."

"That's okay," the girl said. Then she shrugged. "I don't even have a dog."

A Story for

October 20

Lucky Snoopy

Halloween was Snoopy's favorite holiday. This Halloween, he was dressed up as a World War I Flying Ace. He wore a red scarf, goggles, and a cap. He got a lot of looks everywhere he and Charlie Brown went. But Snoopy didn't mind. He loved being the center of attention!

Soon Snoopy and Charlie Brown saw someone walking down the street in a ghost costume. A cloud of dirt swirled at the ghost's feet.

"Happy Halloween, Pigpen," Charlie Brown said.

"How did you know it was me?" Pigpen asked.

Soon Lucy arrived, dressed as a witch, and the four of them set off to go trick-or-treating together.

They walked up to the first house and rang the doorbell. A grown-up opened the door.

"Trick or treat!" Charlie Brown, Lucy, and Pigpen said.

Woof! Snoopy barked.

The grown-up dropped treats into their bags one by one.

Once they were back on the sidewalk, Lucy peered inside her bag. "Awesome, I got a lollipop!" she said.

"I got a piece of chocolate," Pigpen said.

Snoopy looked inside his bag, beaming. He pulled out three giant candy bars.

At the next house, Lucy got a stick of gum. Pigpen got taffy.

Meanwhile, Snoopy received five peanut butter treats *and* taffy *and* gum!

"That's not fair," Lucy complained. "Snoopy is just a dog! And he doesn't even say 'trick or treat' or 'thank you!'"

I'm more than just a dog, Snoopy thought. *I'm the famous World War I Flying Ace!*

As they went from house to house, Snoopy always received the most candy.

Finally, after a girl gave Snoopy two full handfuls of gumdrops, Lucy couldn't stand it anymore.

"Why did you give him more candy than me?" she demanded.

"Are you kidding?" the girl said. "Just look at him! That's the best costume I've ever seen. I almost thought he was a real dog!"

"Good grief," Charlie Brown mumbled.

Snoopy just clutched his full treat bag and giggled.

It happened over and over again. Snoopy got the most candy at every house they went to.

"It's not fair," Lucy repeated.

Snoopy just shrugged. *What can I say?* he thought. *I'm just a lucky dog!*

October 21

Sally Loves Nicknames

One Halloween, Sally agreed to wait for the Great Pumpkin with Linus in the pumpkin patch.

She was thrilled. Of course, Sally would have been thrilled to do absolutely anything with Linus. She thought Linus was wonderful!

"So now that we are here, what do we do?" she asked Linus.

"We just sit and wait," Linus said.

"Okay," Sally said. "What time is he coming?"

"I have no idea," Linus said. "He could come in five minutes or five hours."

Sally was a little confused when she heard that. "Why couldn't we have gone trick-or-treating first, and then come to the pumpkin patch?" she asked.

"Because then we might have missed him," Linus explained. "We have to be here all Halloween night and wait. To show we really believe in him."

Sally smiled. "Okay, my Sweet Babboo," she said. "We'll wait."

Linus sighed. "Thank you, Sally. But I'm not your Sweet Babboo."

Sally smiled to herself. *That's what you think,* she thought.

"Linus, what's your favorite color?" she asked.

Linus thought for a moment. "I'm not sure," he said. "Maybe green. I like green a lot. Why do you ask?"

Sally shrugged. "Well, Christmas will be here soon. I was just thinking about what type of present I was going to get for you."

Linus was embarrassed. "Sally, please. You don't have to buy me a gift." Then he smiled at her and added, "Your presence here tonight is present enough!"

Sally gave Linus a big hug.

"Oh, thank you, my Sweet Babboo!" she gushed.

"Sally, I am not your Sweet Babboo," Linus repeated. "Please stop calling me that."

Sally sighed. When would Linus realize they were destined to be together? Then she had a thought. Maybe he does realize it, but he's just being shy! That was it! He was just too shy to admit he liked her too!

Sally gave Linus another quick squeeze.

"Okay, Punkin!" she said.

A Story for
October 22

Halloween Crush

Charlie Brown remembered last year's Halloween party. Everyone was having a great time. Some kids were bobbing for apples, some kids were dancing, some kids were decorating pumpkins.

Suddenly, Charlie Brown spotted the little red-haired girl on the other side of the room by the punch bowl. Her back was to him, but he could see her beautiful red hair.

He gasped. She was wearing a princess outfit and a tiara.

"Look, there's that little red-haired girl," Charlie Brown whispered to Linus. "She looks even prettier than usual."

"You'll never find a better time to talk to her," Linus said. "Go say something to her now!"

"What should I say?" Charlie Brown asked. He was suddenly nervous. "You know I'm not very good at starting conversations, Linus. Especially around the little red-haired girl. Whenever I try to talk to her, my mind goes blank. I get tongue-tied."

"Just say hi," Linus said. "Play it cool. Just act natural. You just told me you thought she looked pretty, right? Compliment her on her costume."

Charlie Brown decided to take Linus's advice. He would start a nice conversation with the little red-haired girl. He slowly approached the punch bowl and took a deep breath.

Linus is right, Charlie Brown thought. *What do I have to lose?*

Then he tapped the little red-haired girl on the shoulder.

"Excuse me," Charlie Brown said. "I just wanted to tell you I really like your costume. But you look like a princess every day to me."

The girl turned around, and it was Peppermint Patty wearing a red wig! She gave Charlie Brown a huge smile.

"Gee, thanks, Chuck," she said. "Ha! Wait until I tell Marcie. I always knew you liked me, you sly dog!"

Charlie Brown gulped. Not only did he not get a chance to talk to the little red-haired girl, but now Peppermint Patty was convinced he liked *her*!

Good grief!

October 23

Halloween Means Naturally Curly Hair

Last Halloween, Frieda decided to be a fairy princess. She was going to wear a glittery purple gown and a silver crown.

"The crown will go perfectly with my naturally curly hair," she said excitedly.

After she was finished getting ready to go to Lucy's Halloween party, Frieda heard a knock on the door. It was her friend Violet.

"Hi, Frieda!" Violet said. "I love your costume!"

"I love yours, too!" Frieda replied.

Violet was dressed as a scary vampire!

The girls headed over to Lucy's house for the Halloween party. All of their friends were there. Franklin was dressed as a magician, and Charlie Brown was a superhero.

"Okay, everyone!" Lucy suddenly shouted. "Time for Halloween games! We're going to bob for apples. You have ten seconds to try and grab one."

Violet was excited to play. "Frieda, let's do it!" she said. "My giant fangs will definitely give me an advantage."

Frieda tried to imagine playing. She imagined putting her head in the barrel and coming up with her wonderful naturally curly hair soaking wet, dripping all over her beautiful costume.

"No, I'm sorry. It looks like fun, but I can't play," she said sadly.

Suddenly, Franklin had an idea. He took off his magician hat and placed it on the ground.

"Hocus pocus!" he said.

A few moments later, he lifted it up. A giant purple bow had magically appeared underneath the hat!

"Here, Frieda," Franklin said. "You can cover your hair with this bow!"

Frieda didn't know how Franklin's magic spell had worked, but she didn't care. Now she could bob for apples and not get her beautiful curls all wet!

"Thanks, Franklin!" Frieda said. "I love the bow. And it's even purple to match my costume!"

A Story for
October 24

And the Winner Is . . .

Charlie Brown wanted to enter the costume contest at Violet's Halloween party. He was determined to put together a fantastic costume and win!

But what should he dress up as? A ghost? A big, scary monster? What about a baseball player? That would be really easy, since he already had a uniform, cap, and gloves. But then he thought his friends would probably tease him because he wasn't a very good baseball player in real life.

Charlie Brown decided to ask Snoopy because Snoopy loved to dress up. "Snoopy, what should I wear to Violet's Halloween party?"

Snoopy pulled out a big trunk with lots of costumes. After rejecting a bunch of them, he pulled out an oddly shaped hat with a feather.

"You want me to be a pirate?" Charlie Brown said, surprised. But then he thought about it. "I like it!" he said.

Snoopy nodded happily.

But as the party drew nearer, Charlie Brown wasn't sure about his pirate costume. He kept trying new things—he added a puffy shirt, a long velvet jacket, and boots. But it still didn't seem special enough.

When the night of the party finally arrived, Charlie Brown walked over to Snoopy's doghouse for one last look. Snoopy was there with his best friend, Woodstock. They both looked Charlie Brown's costume up and down.

Something is missing, Snoopy thought.

Then Woodstock chirped excitedly to Snoopy. He had an idea! Snoopy smiled. Woodstock's idea was perfect!

Charlie Brown entered the Halloween costume contest—and won! What was the difference?

"I couldn't figure out what was missing at first," Charlie Brown said. "But then we realized, every good pirate needs a crew!"

And then he pointed to Snoopy and Woodstock, who were dressed up as pirates too!

They were a winning team!

October 25

Second Chance

Sally had decided to give the Great Pumpkin one more chance. She told Linus she would wait in the pumpkin patch with him on Halloween night.

So what if the Great Pumpkin didn't show up? She would get to spend time alone with her Sweet Babboo, and that meant the world to her.

It was a beautiful starry night. Linus had picked out a spot right in the middle of the pumpkin patch. Sally was pleased to see that her decision had been worth it. She was enjoying spending her time with Linus. They both settled in and waited.

And waited.

And waited.

After a little while, Sally heard kids laughing in the distance.

"Do you hear that? I hear people laughing," she said to Linus.

Linus looked a little uncomfortable. "Yes, you sometimes can hear kids trick-or-treating."

"Oh," Sally said.

Then they were both quiet again for a while. Then Sally heard something else.

"Now I hear music," she said.

Linus squirmed. "That's probably music from Violet's house," he told her. "She usually plays the music pretty loud."

The music was the last straw for Sally!

She stood up angrily and exclaimed, "I tried, Linus, I really tried. I wanted to stay here with you and wait for the Great Pumpkin. But Halloween only comes once a year. And Violet throws the best parties. She has games and dancing and pizza! I just can't do it! I'm leaving!"

And with that, Sally rushed off, leaving Linus in the pumpkin patch alone.

Linus didn't know what to say. He couldn't promise that the Great Pumpkin was going to show up because he wasn't actually sure.

In desperation he yelled out the only thing he could think of that might work. "Sally, come back! You . . . you can call me your Sweet Babboo!"

A Story for

October 26

Check It Out!

This Halloween, Linus had convinced Snoopy and Woodstock to join him in the pumpkin patch.

Linus didn't mind staying by himself, but sometimes it did get lonely. Besides, he wanted to spread the word about the Great Pumpkin, so it would be great if other people were with him when he finally did show up!

"Make yourselves comfortable," Linus said to Snoopy and Woodstock. "We may be here all night."

Snoopy stretched out in the grass, and Woodstock perched on top of his stomach. They enjoyed the beauty of the empty pumpkin patch.

This is nice, Snoopy thought to himself. *No wonder Linus comes here every Halloween. I could get used to this peace and quiet.*

Woodstock was a different story. He was chirping at Snoopy constantly.

When is the Great Pumpkin coming? How long do we have to stay here? Are we going to miss the big Halloween party?

Snoopy shrugged. He had no idea. He just knew he wanted to support his friend Linus.

Snoopy wished Woodstock would just lie back and relax, so he patted him on the head and told him to calm down.

Woodstock let out a long sigh. He'd do anything for Snoopy, and he did like Linus. But this pumpkin patch was definitely b-o-r-i-n-g.

Linus was looking around thoughtfully. After a minute he spoke.

"I don't know," he said nervously. "I just don't know. This pumpkin patch is so huge." He pointed to one section in the distance. "The Great Pumpkin could be sitting there right now! How would we know? And what if he doesn't see us? Maybe he won't even know we're here. And how will we ever see him?"

We're not going to miss him, Snoopy thought to himself.

He tapped Linus on the shoulder. Linus looked down and saw both Snoopy and Woodstock had binoculars around their necks!

We came prepared, Snoopy thought. *Come on, Great Pumpkin! Show yourself! We are ready for you!*

October 27

Let's Cheer Up Linus

One Halloween night, Snoopy and Woodstock decided to go to the pumpkin patch to check on Linus.

Linus was alone, and he was shivering a little bit. He had wrapped his blanket around himself in order to stay warm, but it wasn't really helping.

He was glad to see his friends though. "I thought for sure this was the year, guys," Linus said.

Snoopy and Woodstock both looked around and nodded, although they weren't exactly sure what Linus meant by "the most sincere pumpkin patch you've ever seen." Pumpkin patches all looked the same to them!

"I sat here thinking about everyone out trick-or-treating," Linus told Snoopy and Woodstock.

He paused and then he continued, "I wondered if you were all having fun and getting lots of candy. Then I thought about the big Halloween party at Violet's house. I wondered if everyone wore great costumes and danced and bobbed for apples.

"But then I thought about the Great Pumpkin, and I knew when he showed up, it would be worth the wait. Finally seeing the Great Pumpkin would be better than any Halloween candy or party or costume."

Then Linus fell silent for a moment again.

"But he never showed up," he said sadly.

Snoopy and Woodstock felt terrible for their friend. Snoopy grabbed Linus's hand and looked up at him with big, sad eyes. Snoopy then looked over at Woodstock.

What can we do to make Linus feel better? Snoopy wondered.

It was as if Linus could read Snoopy's mind. "Thank you, Snoopy for your concern," he said. "But I'm so sad. I don't think anything would make me feel better right now."

Suddenly, Woodstock began chirping excitedly to Snoopy.

Snoopy smiled at Woodstock. He nodded.

Then they both wrapped Linus in the biggest hug ever! And they wouldn't let go!

"You know what, guys?" Linus said. "I do feel better! Thanks!"

October 28

A Scary Costume

Snoopy and Woodstock were trying to make Linus laugh and forget about the Great Pumpkin. Snoopy was great at doing impressions, so he acted out the reactions he and Woodstock got while trick-or-treating.

First, he was a grumpy old man. Then he imitated a sweet old lady who gave them lots of treats. Finally, he imitated the house that had six cats—both Snoopy and Woodstock had run away in a hurry!

"It sounds like you both had a lot of fun, even with all the cats," Linus said.

Both Snoopy and Woodstock nodded happily. Linus realized that neither one of them had a costume on.

"Hey, what did you dress up as?" he asked.

Woodstock flew into his treat bag for a moment and pulled out a Snoopy costume. He put it on to show Linus.

"That's great—you look like a mini Snoopy!" Linus turned to the real Snoopy and said, "He could be your little brother," which made both Snoopy and Woodstock laugh really hard! "And what about you, Snoopy? What did you dress up as? Did you dress up as Woodstock?"

Snoopy shook his head no, but he smiled at Woodstock. *That would have been a good idea!* he told Woodstock, making him giggle.

"So if you weren't Woodstock, what did you dress up as? Did you dress up as something scary?"

Snoopy nodded.

"Really scary?" Linus asked.

Snoopy nodded yes again.

"A monster? A ghost? A vampire bat?" Linus guessed.

Snoopy and Woodstock both shook their heads no to all those things.

"Okay, I give up. What did you dress up as that was scarier than monsters, ghosts, or vampire bats?" Linus said.

Snoopy turned around for a moment. When he turned back and faced Linus, his ears were all curled up and he had a very crabby look on his face. He looked just like Linus's sister Lucy when she was mad!

Linus laughed. "You're right Snoopy—there's nothing scarier than Lucy when she's angry!"

October 29

Lucy and Rerun Are the Best!

The day after Halloween, Linus didn't want to get out of bed because he didn't want anyone to ask, "Sooo, how was the Great Pumpkin? Did you get lots of presents?"

Linus groaned and pulled the covers over his head. He wished he could stay in bed all day. He wished he could stay in bed all week!

Just then, his sister Lucy poked her head into his room. "Mom told me to make sure you get up," she said. "Or you'll be late for school."

Linus sighed. "Fine," he said and sat up in bed. He looked over at Lucy. He was waiting for her to make a joke about the Great Pumpkin. "Well?"

"Well, what?" Lucy asked. "Why are you looking at me like that? Hurry up and get dressed!" Then Lucy ran out of his room.

Hmmm, Linus thought. *That was odd.* He wondered if Lucy was up to something.

As Linus brushed his teeth, he started to feel a little sad again. He thought about all the fun he missed, especially trick-or-treating. Not only did he not get to dress up and hang out with his friends, but he also didn't get any candy!

Did Lucy and Rerun get lots of treats? It was going to be awful watching both of them enjoy it all. He wondered if they would share any of it with him. Probably not.

Linus then remembered that before she went trick-or-treating,

Lucy had said to him, "Don't expect us to get any candy for you."

He got dressed and rushed down the stairs. It was a little late, so he'd have to hurry through his breakfast.

As he ran into the kitchen, he stopped short. Next to his cereal bowl was a big Halloween trick-or-treat bag. He peeked inside. It was filled with candy!

"Surprise!" someone yelled.

Linus turned around. Lucy and Rerun were there, smiling at him.

"You didn't really think we'd forget about you, did you?" Lucy said.

"Happy day after Halloween!" Rerun shouted.

It was the best day after Halloween ever!

A Story for

October 30

Never Give Up!

The week before Halloween, Linus invited all of his friends at school to come sit with him in the pumpkin patch to wait for the Great Pumpkin, but they all turned him down.

While walking home, Linus ran into Peppermint Patty.

"Hey, Linus, why do you look so glum?" she asked.

"No one believes in the Great Pumpkin," Linus told her.

"What's a Great Pumpkin?" Peppermint Patty asked.

Linus's eyes lit up. He told Peppermint Patty all about the Great Pumpkin and how he brought children presents and warm autumn wishes.

Peppermint Patty perked up at the word "presents."

"The Great Pumpkin brings presents?" she repeated. "Really?"

"Yes," Linus said.

"I'm in!" Peppermint Patty said. "See you on Halloween, Linus!"

On Halloween night, Peppermint Patty sat in the pumpkin patch with Linus. "I can't wait for my new baseball glove," Peppermint Patty said. "That's what I told the Great Pumpkin I wanted."

"You told him what to bring you?" Linus shouted. "Now he'll never come! Leave this pumpkin patch right now!"

Linus was alone in the pumpkin patch. And once again, the Great Pumpkin never showed up.

The next day he apologized to Peppermint Patty. "I'm sorry I yelled at you last night," he said.

Peppermint Patty smiled. "It's okay. And cheer up, there's always next year."

Linus shook his head. "Maybe it's time for me to stop believing."

Marcie walked over to Linus. "Don't stop believing, Linus," she said. "Believing makes you a dreamer. And that's a great thing! The world needs more dreamers."

Suddenly, Linus felt better. "Thanks so much, Marcie," he said.

"And who knows?" Marcie continued. "Maybe the Great Zucchini will show up next year!"

October 31

The Great Pumpkin Exists!

Another Halloween had come and gone. Linus looked around the pumpkin patch. He felt a little pang of sadness when he thought about the trick-or-treating and other fun he had missed. But even though he thought for sure this was going to be the year he would see the Great Pumpkin, Linus would not let himself be discouraged. There was always next year.

Linus shivered. It was getting late and cold. It was time for him to head home. He gave the pumpkin patch one last look. Why hadn't the Great Pumpkin come? Was there really a more sincere pumpkin patch than this one?

Linus sighed. All the kids would ask him about the Great Pumpkin, and he would have to admit he never came. Again.

Then something caught his eye. Linus saw that it was a small, shiny Halloween bag with a smiling pumpkin on it and a tag with his name.

He peeked inside the bag, and he saw his favorite candy bar and a note:

Dear Linus,

Happy Halloween.

Love,

The Great Pumpkin

Linus quickly looked around. He was alone, but . . . the Great Pumpkin came! He left him his favorite candy bar! It was the greatest Halloween ever! He couldn't wait to tell Charlie Brown, Lucy, Rerun, and the rest of his friends. He smiled all the way home.

Linus was so happy he never noticed Snoopy and Woodstock hiding behind a huge pumpkin. When Linus was gone, Snoopy and Woodstock looked at each other and smiled. Then they high-fived.

Mission accomplished, Snoopy thought.

They were so happy they were able to make their friend happy. It really was the best Halloween ever!